TARZAN®
OF THE
APES

By Edgar Rice Burroughs

Adapted by Harold and Geraldine Woods

Text illustrations by Tim Gaydos

Step into Classics™

Random House ⌂ New York

"Tarzan of the Apes" abridged and adapted by Random House, Inc. Copyright © 1982 Edgar Rice Burroughs, Inc.

Cover illustration by Angelo. Copyright © 1997 Edgar Rice Burroughs, Inc.

Interior illustrations by Tim Gaydos. Copyright © 1982 Edgar Rice Burroughs, Inc.

http://www.randomhouse.com/

Library of Congress Cataloging-in-Publication Data
Woods, Harold.
Tarzan of the Apes. (Step into classics)
SUMMARY: Tarzan, born in the jungle and raised by apes, comes to America.
ISBN 0-394-85089-0 (pbk.) — 0-394-95089-5 (lib. bdg.)
[1. Jungles—Fiction] I. Woods, Geraldine. II. Gaydos, Tim, ill.
III. Burroughs, Edgar Rice, 1875–1950. Tarzan of the apes. IV. Title.
V. Series
PZ7.W8636Tar [Fic] 81-19873

Printed in the United States of America 14 13 12 11 10 9 8 7 6 5

CHAPTER ONE

Once there was a young nobleman from England. I will call him John Clayton. He was the Lord of Greystoke. He was sent to Africa by his government. His young wife, Alice, went with him. She was Lady Greystoke.

They sailed over the ocean for many weeks. Their first stop was North Africa. From there they traveled south on another boat called the *Fuwalda*. The *Fuwalda*'s captain was an evil man. He often beat his crew. Once he even tried to shoot a sailor named Black Michael. John Clayton stopped him. Black Michael was thankful for Clayton's help.

Later there was more trouble. Black Michael and the other crew members killed the captain. They took over the ship. During the battle Lord and Lady Greystoke stayed in their cabin. They were afraid for their lives.

Finally the fighting stopped. John Clayton and his wife came on deck. A horrible sight met their eyes. Bodies lay all around. The rebel sailors were throwing the dead and wounded into the sea.

Suddenly a sailor saw the Claytons. "Here's two more for the fishes!" he cried. He ran toward them. An ax was in his hand.

But Black Michael was quicker

with his gun. The sailor went down with a bullet in his back. Black Michael put his smoking gun down. He roared, "These are my friends! They are to be left alone!

"Keep to your cabin," he then said to Lord Greystoke. "No one will hurt you there."

The Claytons were happy to do as he asked. For five days they stayed in their cabin. From time to time they heard fighting on deck. Gunshots rang out twice. Finally Black Michael sent for them. "We have reached land," he said. "You must go ashore. You are not safe on this ship. The other sailors think you will make trouble for us. They want to kill you."

"You cannot do that!" cried Lord

Greystoke. "This is a wild jungle. There is no one to help us here!"

But Black Michael would not listen. "I will give you supplies," he said. "You will be all right. I will tell people where to find you. They will come to pick you up."

John Clayton knew that Black Michael was lying. The sailor would not tell anyone where they were. But he also knew Black Michael would not change his mind. Clayton went to his cabin to pack his bags.

The next morning the sailors put a small boat into the water. Inside were many boxes. They held food, pots and pans, old sails, and books. Then the sailors rowed the Claytons ashore. All of the boxes were dumped on the beach. With frightened eyes the Claytons watched the sailors leave.

The Claytons stood silently for a few minutes. They could hear the cries of savage beasts behind them in the jungle. After a while Alice said, "Oh, John! The horror of it! If it were only you and I. But the baby. . . . What will we do when the baby comes?"

"Don't worry," he said. "Our great-great-grandparents lived in forests. We have better tools. We will survive. And so will the child."

Then John Clayton set to work. His first job was to build a safe place for them to sleep. By nightfall he was finished. He had made a tree house. Once inside, the Claytons tried to sleep. But terrible sounds kept them

up all night. They heard wild cries and the sound of huge animals beneath their house. Lord Greystoke finally fell asleep near the door. A gun lay next to his hand.

In the morning John Clayton began work on a cabin. It took more than a month to finish. When it was done, the couple felt safer. Four strong walls protected them now. A heavy door and a lock shut out the wild world. Inside, a table, chairs, and a bed made them comfortable. The Claytons began to relax. They soon forgot how dangerous wild animals could be.

One afternoon John was working in the jungle. All at once the monkeys in the trees above him ran away. He looked around quickly. A great ape was coming toward him. The beast was growling savagely. What could he do? The monster was clearly stronger than he. All of his guns were in the cabin. "Go inside, Alice!" he cried. "Lock the door! I will kill this ape with my ax!"

But he knew he was facing a horrible death. And so did Alice.

The ape weighed three hundred pounds or more. His eyes were filled with hatred. With an ugly growl he faced Clayton.

Alice came out of the cabin. She held a gun.

"Alice! Go back!" screamed Clayton. Just then the animal charged. Clayton swung his ax. But the beast grabbed it and threw it away. He dropped his heavy arms around

Clayton. His head came forward, ready to bite. As his teeth reached Clayton's neck, Alice shot the ape.

But the bullet did not kill the animal right away. The ape threw Clayton to the ground. Then he turned toward Alice. She tried to fire again. But she did not know how to reload the gun! The beast jumped on her. Then he fell to the ground. The ape was dead.

Clayton ran to his wife. She had fainted. But she was not harmed.

The ape had died as he jumped. He had not had time to hurt her.

Clayton carried his wife to the cabin. That night their son was born. He was strong and healthy.

But Lady Alice never got over the ape's attack. She took good care of the baby. But her mind was never the same.

"I had a bad dream, John," she said one morning. "I dreamed I was in the jungle. I'm so glad I woke up. It is wonderful to be in England." John tried to explain. But it did no good.

On her son's first birthday, Lady Alice died. Clayton's heart was broken. He could not believe his wife was gone. Sadly he took out his diary. He had written in it every day. This was the last thing he wrote: "My little son is crying for food. Oh, Alice, Alice, what shall I do?"

Then he put his head on his arms. He stayed that way for a long time. The jungle was deathly quiet. There was only one sound to be heard—the cries of a little baby.

CHAPTER TWO

About a mile from the Claytons' cabin lived a great ape. His name was Kerchak. He was the king of a large tribe of apes. On the day that Lady Greystoke died, Kerchak was very angry.

None of the apes knew why Kerchak was angry. And no one wanted to stay to find out. When Kerchak was angry, he was very dangerous! The apes ran away from him. The youngest climbed to the treetops. One of them took a bad step. She crashed to the forest floor. Kerchak screamed and jumped on her. He crushed her head with a branch.

Then Kala the ape appeared. She was carrying a little baby on her back. Kala had been looking for food. She did not know that Kerchak was angry. After one look she ran up a tree. Kerchak followed. To get away, Kala had to take a chance. She jumped from one tree to another. The two trees were far apart. Kala made it. But her baby did not. The sudden movement made him lose his grip. He fell to the forest floor.

Kala was horrified. She raced down and picked up the little ape. He was dead. Kala hugged the body and began to cry.

After that, Kerchak calmed down. He gave an order to the tribe. They were going to the sea. Kerchak had seen a cabin on the beach. All of the apes had seen it. They had also seen the strange hairless apes that lived inside. Many of the Kerchak's tribe had been killed by the strange apes. Kerchak hated them!

Kala went with the others. But she was still very sad. She did not want to put her dead baby down. She carried his body all the way to the sea.

Soon the apes arrived at the cabin. They were surprised. The door was open. Very quietly they walked inside. There they saw the strange ape. He was sitting with his head in his hands. A body was lying on the bed. In a cradle a baby was crying.

For one moment Kerchak stood still. Then John Clayton looked up.

Kerchak charged! He killed Clayton with one blow.

Then Kerchak turned toward the baby. But Kala was too quick for him. She dropped her own dead child. Then she grabbed the live one. She ran out the door carrying the baby boy.

Kerchak and the other apes rushed out of the cabin too. As they did, the door shut. The lock clicked. They tried to get back inside. But they did not know how to open the door. The cabin was closed to them forever.

Outside Kala held the crying baby tightly. She was an ape, but she was also a mother. Kala knew what the baby needed. She offered him her milk. The child felt her mother's love. He quieted down and began to drink. At that moment he became her son.

Kala named her baby Tarzan. In ape language, Tarzan means "white skin." The other apes thought Tarzan was ugly. He did not have thick fur. He was not as strong as the other ape children. Why, it took him almost a year to learn how to walk! The other ape babies walked when they were two months old. But Kala loved little Tarzan. She cared for him as if he were her own son.

Nine years passed. Tarzan was still only a boy. But what a boy! His mother had taught him to swing through the jungle. He never missed a branch! He could climb the tallest tree like a squirrel. He could drop back to the ground with amazing speed. Tarzan was stronger than a twenty-year-old man. He was a better climber and runner than any person alive.

Tarzan was happy with the apes. He did not know he was human. He remembered no other home. For Tarzan there was no world but the jungle.

Then one day Tarzan saw what he looked like. He and a young ape were drinking water from a lake. Tarzan looked in the water. He was shocked. His face was not the same as his friend's. His nose was thin. His eyes were pale. His skin looked bare and shiny. Tarzan turned red with shame. He could think of nothing but how ugly he was. He was so upset that he didn't hear Sabor.

Sabor was a huge lioness. All the animals in the jungle feared her. Now she was right behind Tarzan. She was ready to jump—and kill.

Tarzan and his friend went on drinking water. Then they heard a savage roar. They turned around. Sabor was attacking them! The ape was afraid. He could not move. It was easy for the lioness to kill him.

But Tarzan was different. His life in the jungle had made him fast. And his human brain could think. The second he heard Sabor's roar, Tarzan looked around. Behind him was a deadly lion. In front of him was water. Sabor could not swim. Neither could Tarzan. However, the water looked more appealing than the lion. Tarzan jumped in.

He sank to the bottom of the lake. Most people would have panicked. Most people would have drowned. But Tarzan was braver than most people. He moved his hands, as if to climb a tree. That made him rise to the top. He kept moving his hands. He stayed on top of the water. Tarzan was very happy. He had learned to swim!

Sabor waited on the shore. However, Tarzan did not come near her. Instead he gave the ape cry for help. The tribe heard it. They hurried to the lake. When Sabor saw them, she ran away. Then Tarzan swam to shore. From that day on he swam whenever he got the chance. The other apes were amazed. They did not like to swim.

As Tarzan grew he learned other things. Everything he learned made him different from the other apes. One day he learned to make ropes out of grass. He practiced hunting with them. None of his friends could do that.

Tarzan was also very curious. He knew about the cabin on the beach. His ape friends stayed away from it. They knew they could not get inside. But that did not stop Tarzan. He went to it often. He climbed on the roof. He poked at the windows. How much he wanted to find a way in!

One day he noticed something strange on the door. It was the lock his father had made long ago. Of course, Tarzan did not know that. He played with it anyway. He tapped and turned it. Finally it opened! Tarzan went inside the cabin.

The bones of John and Alice Clayton were there. So was the skeleton of Kala's baby. Tarzan paid no attention to them. He was a hunter. He was used to bodies and bones. And he had no idea they were the bones of his parents. Besides, other things interested him more.

One was a knife. Tarzan picked it up. He had never seen such a thing. He cut his finger. But he did not mind. The cut showed him what the knife was for. He practiced cutting bits of paper and wood.

Then he looked at the books. He had no idea what they were. He could not read or write. In fact, he did not even speak much. His few words were in ape language, not English.

Some of the books had many pictures. One was an alphabet book. Tarzan saw a picture of a hairless ape inside. The ape looked like Tarzan. He also saw monkeys, a lion, and a snake. Under the big pictures were tiny pictures. They were all black. They looked like bugs. Most of them had legs, but none had eyes and mouths. Tarzan thought the bugs were interesting. He did not know they were letters!

Tarzan studied the little bugs. He learned that some bugs were always under the same picture. The bugs "BOY" were with the little hairless ape. "LION" was under Sabor's picture.

Tarzan began to understand what the little bugs were for. They were words.

Then one day he found a pencil. He practiced using it on the table. After a while he learned to make the bugs himself.

Tarzan studied whenever he had the chance. He did not learn everything at once. It took him many years. By the time he was seventeen, he could read and write. But he could not speak. He had never heard a human talk.

Tarzan kept on working. There were many books in his parents' cabin. Tarzan wanted to read them all. He also practiced using the knife. It helped protect him in the wild jungle.

CHAPTER THREE

Tarzan learned an important thing from reading. He learned that he was not an ape. He was another kind of animal—a man. Now Tarzan knew why he had no fur. He did not feel ugly anymore. But Tarzan still stayed with his tribe. They were like a family to him.

Life in the jungle was interesting. There were fish to catch and animals to hunt. Sometimes the animals hunted Tarzan! But that was no problem for the boy. Sabor and her friends were fast. But Tarzan was faster than lightning. He could always get away.

Then one day everything changed. People came to the jungle. They walked through the forest in a long line. There were many warriors and their families. Each warrior carried a spear and a long bow. Tied to each man's belt was a bunch of poison arrows.

These people were native Africans. They were looking for a place to make a new village. They could not stay in their old home anymore. Traders from Europe had wanted rubber and ivory from them. The Africans did not want to trade. They wanted to be left alone. But the Europeans did not give up. Finally the Africans fought the Europeans. But the Africans lost the battle. So they had to move on.

For three days the tribe marched. Then their chief told them to stop. Soon the people built a new village.

About three miles away lived Tarzan's tribe of apes. For a while there was no trouble. But one day a young African named Kulonga went for a walk. He got hungry and shot an animal with his poison arrows. It was Kala, Tarzan's mother. But Kulonga never had his meal. The other apes arrived, and Kulonga ran for his life.

Tarzan came quickly when he heard the apes' cries. He found the tribe standing by Kala's body. He could not believe what he saw. Kala, his mother, dead! Anger and sadness filled his soul. He wanted to

destroy Kala's killer.

The apes told him that another ape

with no fur was the killer. They showed him where Kulonga had gone. Tarzan did not wait. Quickly he ran through the jungle. He could follow Kulonga's trail easily. But something made his heart beat faster. The track's of Kala's killer looked like Tarzan's tracks. Could her killer be a man?

After he had gone about a mile, Tarzan saw Kulonga. The man was holding his bow and arrow. He was about to shoot a wild pig. Tarzan wanted to kill Kulonga right away. But Tarzan waited. He was curious. This was the first man he had ever seen. Tarzan sat in a tree and watched Kulonga.

Kulonga shot only one arrow. It hit the pig in the neck. Tarzan thought the pig would keep running. Its wound was very tiny. But the pig fell dead right away. Tarzan had never heard of poison. But he knew there was something special about Kulonga's arrows. He wanted some to hunt with.

As Tarzan watched, Kulonga built a fire. He cut meat from the pig and cooked it. Tarzan was surprised. The apes had seen fire only a few times. It came with Ara, the lightning. Tarzan wondered why the man put the meat in the fire. Perhaps he was sharing it with Ara?

After he ate, Kulonga went to sleep in a tree. Tarzan hid in the same tree. When Kulonga woke up, his bow and arrows were gone. Tarzan had taken them. Kulonga was afraid. He was alone in the wild jungle. He had nothing to fight with.

Kulonga began to run toward the village. Tarzan followed. He wanted to see where Kulonga lived. Soon Kulonga was at the village gate. But he did not get a chance to go in. Tarzan threw his rope around Kulonga's neck. He pulled hard. Kulonga rose in the air. Then Tarzan stabbed him with his knife. "For Kala," he said in ape language.

Now Tarzan looked at the village. He knew there were many men inside. He wanted to see other animals like himself. But he could not let the natives see him. They might think he was an enemy. So Tarzan climbed a tree next to the village wall. Carefully he went out on a long branch. No one saw him. No one heard him. He was as quiet as Sabor the lioness.

Tarzan looked down. A woman was there. She was stirring something in a pot. After a while she dipped some arrows into the pot. Then she put the arrows on the ground. Tarzan knew they were like Kulonga's arrows.

Suddenly a native shouted. He was pointing to Kulonga's body. All of the people began to run to him. Tarzan saw his chance. In two seconds he climbed down the tree. He picked up the arrows. Then he kicked the pot of poison. It spilled on the ground. In two more seconds he was back in the jungle.

Tarzan was very busy during the next month. He practiced every day with his bow and arrow. Soon he was a good shot. When he needed more arrows, he went back to the village. He always waited until all of the natives were away. They never found out who was taking their arrows.

Tarzan also visited his parents' cabin often. One day he found a metal box there. In it was a locket. It was his mother's. Under the locket was a book. The book was John Clayton's diary. It was written in French. Tarzan had never seen French.

Tarzan tried to read the book. But he could not understand the words. That made him angry. He knew this book was special. All of the other books were on a shelf. This one was in a box. "Someday," thought Tarzan, "I will learn the secret of this book."

Tarzan started for home. He stopped to eat some berries. When he looked up, Sabor was there. Tarzan took out an arrow. As the lion jumped, Tarzan shot. The arrow hit Sabor in the chest. But still she jumped right on top of Tarzan. They fell to the ground. Tarzan grabbed his knife. Sabor's heavy body was on top of him. It was hard to lift his

arm! With super strength, Tarzan stabbed. Sabor roared once more . . . and died. Tarzan slid out from under Sabor. He put his foot on her body He gave the ape victory cry.

The apes heard him. They came to see what had happened. Proudly Tarzan said, "See what I have done. I am Tarzan, mighty hunter. No one is braver than I."

The apes looked at Sabor's huge body. One said, "A strong enemy is dead. The tribe is glad."

But Kerchak, the King of the Apes, was not glad. His eyes were filled with hate. "I am the bravest!" he screamed.

Kerchak could see the apes did not believe it. He went crazy with anger. He roared, "Tarzan, great killer! Come and fight me! I am greater than you!"

Tarzan faced Kerchak. He was tired from the fight with Sabor. And Kerchak would be hard to beat. The old ape was almost seven feet tall. His shoulders were round with huge muscles. His neck was as hard as iron. But Tarzan would not run from the fight.

As Kerchak charged, Tarzan drew his knife. He pushed it into Kerchak's body. Before Tarzan could pull the knife out, Kerchak grabbed it. He threw the knife away! Now Tarzan had no weapon to fight with.

Kerchak aimed a blow at Tarzan's head. If he had hit Tarzan, Kerchak would have killed him. But Tarzan ducked. Then he slammed his fist into Kerchak's stomach. The ape almost fell. The blood was dripping from his wound. But still he grabbed Tarzan. His long teeth bent toward Tarzan's neck. Tarzan tried to push Kerchak away. The young man was an inch from death! But finally Kerchak gave up. He slid to the ground, dead.

Tarzan placed his foot on Kerchak's chest. He gave the victory cry. The other apes bowed. Tarzan had killed their king. Now he was the new King of the Apes.

CHAPTER FOUR

Tarzan was the best king the apes ever had. His mind was quick. He helped the apes find food easily. He was also a master hunter. He brought much meat to the tribe. Best of all, he was a good judge. He kept peace in the tribe.

The apes were very happy with Tarzan. But Tarzan was not happy with them. He had learned much from them when he was a child. But now Tarzan was a man. The apes seemed dull to him. He could not tell them his thoughts. They did not understand him. Tarzan wanted to be with other people. He wanted to live in the cabin, like a man.

Tarzan called the apes together. "I am the best hunter," he said.

"Yes," answered the apes. "Tarzan is great."

"But Tarzan," he said, "is not an ape. He is not like you. So Tarzan is going away. He is going to the house of his own people. You must pick another king. Tarzan will not come back."

And so Tarzan ended his life with the apes. He was twenty-one years old. He was more than six feet tall. His body was perfect. His muscles were like iron. His face was very handsome. He looked like a forest god.

However, Tarzan was lonely. He needed other people. He thought of going to the African village. But a man from the village had killed Kala. Tarzan did not think he could make friends there. He had loved his mother too much. So Tarzan stayed alone in his cabin.

But soon other people came. It happened one day while Tarzan was at the forest edge. He could see something strange on the sea. A ship! And on the beach was a small boat. Near the cabin were sailors.

One of the sailors was very short. Tarzan thought he looked like Pamba, the rat. Another sailor was very tall. He was shouting at Rat Face.

Rat Face had a gun in his belt.

He pointed the gun at the big sailor. He made the big sailor turn around. He shot him in the back. Everyone was quiet for a minute. Then the rest of the sailors started laughing. They slapped Rat Face on the back and smiled at him. A few minutes later they all rowed back to the ship.

Tarzan was confused. Was that how men acted? They seemed very cruel. The animals did not laugh as they killed. And Rat Face had shot the other man in the back. Tarzan knew that was wrong. He would have to be careful of Rat Face.

Tarzan went to his cabin. Someone had been there. It was a mess. Books and papers were on the floor. Tarzan was very angry. He ran to the shelf. Thank goodness! The metal box was still there. The book and the locket were safe.

Then Tarzan's quick ears heard a sound. What was it? He looked out of the window. The boat was coming back.

Tarzan grabbed a piece of paper and wrote quickly. He put the note on the door. He took his box and many arrows and spears. Then he hid in the jungle.

Soon the boat landed. The sailors had come back. With them were new people. One was an old man, Professor Porter. A thin young man and a fat older woman were with him. And there was a girl. She was about nineteen and very pretty. Her name was Jane Porter. The young man helped her off the boat.

The group stayed on the beach for a while. The sailors took many boxes off the boat. Then they all walked toward the cabin. Rat Face was first. When he saw Tarzan's note, he stopped. "What's this?" he said.

Rat Face could not read. He turned to the old man. "Professor, take a look at this," he said.

The old man came forward slowly. He looked at the paper. He read:

"THIS IS THE HOUSE OF TARZAN, THE KILLER OF BEASTS. DO NOT HARM TARZAN'S THINGS. TARZAN WATCHES. TARZAN OF THE APES."

"Who is Tarzan?" cried one sailor.

"He must speak English," said the girl. "But why does it say 'of the apes'?"

"I don't know, Miss Porter," said the young man. His name was William Clayton. He was Tarzan's cousin. Of course, he did not know that. Neither did Tarzan.

Rat Face pushed the girl aside. "Let me see that paper," he growled.

William Clayton stopped him with an angry hand. "You killed the captain of our ship. You robbed us. I can't do a thing about that. But if you hurt Jane Porter, I will kill you."

Before Clayton could do anything, Rat Face fired his gun. Jane Porter screamed. But Tarzan had thrown a spear through the sailor's shoulder just in time. Thanks to Tarzan the bullet went wild and Rat Face fell.

William Clayton ran to Jane. They looked toward the jungle. All they saw was a wall of green.

"Who threw the spear?" she whispered. "Who could it have been?"

"Tarzan must be watching," answered Clayton. "He saved my life." Suddenly the young man looked around. His voice was filled with alarm. "Miss Porter!" he cried.

"Where is your father?"

"He walked into the jungle," said the fat woman. She was Esmeralda, Jane's maid. "I think he was looking for food. He must have gotten lost."

Clayton and Jane began to shout for her father. There was no answer. Clayton did not know what to do. Should he go and look for the man? Clayton did not want to leave the women alone with the sailors. However, Mr. Porter was old. Clayton knew he would die in the jungle. He had to find the professor! Then Clayton had an idea. He slipped a gun to Jane.

"Go into the cabin with Esmeralda," he said. "Take the gun. You will be safe there. I will bring your father back."

Jane did as Clayton asked. She ran to the cabin. When she went inside, she saw the bones of Lord and Lady Greystoke. She shook her head sadly. "What a horrible place we are in," she said.

Jane and her maid locked the door. They put their arms around each other and waited.

Clayton headed into the jungle. First he walked one way, then another. As he walked, he called Professor Porter's name. In a few minutes he was lost.

Tarzan followed him. He could not understand what the young man was doing. At first Tarzan thought he was looking for the old man. But the young man had passed the old one's tracks without stopping. Now he was walking toward the native village. Tarzan shook his head. Why would he want to go there? Tarzan knew the jungle so well. He could not imagine anyone being lost there.

Then Tarzan saw Numa the lion. He was trailing the man. "Why doesn't this man do something," thought Tarzan. "Doesn't he hear Numa coming?" Of course, Clayton did not hear the quiet steps. His ears were not used to soft jungle sounds. He kept on walking. He did not know he was on the path of death.

Suddenly Numa stepped in front of Clayton. The man froze. He heard a sound behind him. "Another animal," he thought. "I'm trapped!"

But it was Tarzan behind him. As Numa jumped, so did Tarzan. The ape man landed right on the lion's back. With lightning speed his arm went around Numa's neck. Iron muscles forced the lion into the air. The giant of the jungle held the lion with one hand. With the other he stabbed the lion to death.

"Thank you!" said Clayton. "You saved my life!"

Tarzan did not answer. He did not know how to speak English. He just pointed in the direction of the sea. He had realized that Clayton was lost. He wanted to take Clayton back to the cabin.

They had not gone far when they heard a shot. Tarzan began to run. But Clayton could not keep up. He fell again and again. Clayton never forgot what happened next. Tarzan lifted the young man onto his back. He climbed high into the trees. Then he swung quickly through the forest.

Clayton felt as if he were flying. He could not even see the ground. But he trusted Tarzan. The jungle man knew where he was going. A few minutes later they reached the sea.

They came down so fast that Clayton felt as if they were falling. However, Tarzan landed gently. Then both men ran to the cabin.

They were just in time. They could see a lioness climbing through the window! Her front paws and head were already in. Only her back paws were still outside. There was a small wound in the beast's shoulder. Jane had shot the lioness. But the animal was not badly hurt. Now the two women were helpless. Like Tarzan's mother long ago, they did not know how to reload the gun.

Tarzan would not let them die. He grabbed the lion's tail and pulled. Clayton was behind him. Tarzan said, "Quick! Take my knife. Stab the beast while I hold her!" But Tarzan spoke in ape language. Clayton did not understand. He wanted to help, but he did not know how. So Clayton stayed pressed against the cabin wall, out of the way.

For the second time that day Tarzan fought with a lion. The winner gave a savage victory cry. It was Tarzan.

"What was that sound?" Jane called out. Her voice was full of fear.

"The voice of the man who saved your life," said Clayton. He went into the cabin.

"Oh, Mr. Clayton, I was so scared. The sailors left. There was no one to help. Thank God you came!" cried Jane.

"Do not thank me, Jane," answered Clayton. Then he told her

about the giant man of the jungle. "Come and meet him," he said.

They went outside. Tarzan was standing near the lion's body. He was sweating. Some of the lion's blood was on his arm. But he looked strong and handsome.

Jane did not know what to say. She thought Tarzan was the most wonderful man she had ever seen. And he had saved her life! Her feelings were too strong for words.

Tarzan too was silent. He had learned in his books that this was a "woman." He had never imagined anything so beautiful! If only he could speak with her. But he knew these people did not understand ape language.

At last Jane spoke. "Thank you for

saving us. Will you come inside and rest?"

Tarzan smiled at her. Then he disappeared into the jungle.

CHAPTER FIVE

After saving Jane, Tarzan had many more things to do. First he looked for Jane's father. He had gone in search of food and had gotten lost in the jungle. When Tarzan found him, he was on the beach a few miles from the cabin. Tarzan helped him home. Then Tarzan hurried back into the jungle.

He had seen the ship getting ready to leave. He wanted to see it closely before it sailed. Near the cabin was a good lookout point. Tarzan saw the ship sail north. It stopped about a half-mile from the cabin. Rat Face and some other sailors put a small boat in the water. They lowered a chest into the boat. Then they all jumped in and rowed to shore. Tarzan could see a thick bandage on Rat Face's shoulder.

Now Tarzan was really curious. He waited to see what would happen. Rat Face told the sailors to dig a hole. As they dug, Rat Face spoke. "We can't take this treasure with us," he said. "If we are caught, it will mean trouble. Let's leave it here. We can come back for it later." The men buried the chest. Then they went back to the ship and sailed away.

Tarzan returned to the cabin. He wanted to check on his friends. All were sleeping except Jane. She was writing at a table. The lamp shone on her golden hair. She looked beautiful. Tarzan could not take his eyes off her. Love filled his heart. He was sorry when Jane blew out the lamp. She went to bed.

Tarzan wondered what Jane had been writing. Now he could find out. He reached through the window and took her papers. This is what she had written:

Africa, February 3(?), 1902

Dear Hazel,

It is silly to write a letter you may never see. But I must tell someone what has happened. As you know, we have sailed to Africa. We came to look for treasure. Papa had a map.

Well, we found the treasure. A chest full of gold coins! We started for home. Three days later the sailors on our ship began to fight. They killed our captain. They stole our treasure. Then they left us alone on the shore.

Mr. Clayton is with us. He is the son of Lord Greystoke of England. One day he will be a lord. He's very nice. I think he's in love with me. I don't know if I love him.

We have had many adventures. Papa was lost. Mr. Clayton was attacked by a lion. So were Esmeralda and I. A wonderful person saved all of us. He looks like a forest god. He is strong and brave. But he speaks no English. After he helped us, he disappeared into the forest.

We have another friend, whose name is Tarzan. We are living in his cabin. He put a note on the door. It warned us not to take his things. Strangely, we have never seen him. However, he saved Mr. Clayton's life. One of the sailors was going to shoot Mr. Clayton. Tarzan threw a spear and stopped him.

The sailors didn't leave us much food. We have only three bullets for our gun. We will not be able to hunt many animals. We don't know how we will eat.

I'm tired now. I will say good night.

Love,
Jane Porter

After reading the letter, Tarzan sat thinking. Jane did not know he was Tarzan! And she was worried about food. Well, he would take care of that. From that day on Tarzan hunted food for the strangers. Each day he left fruit or meat by the cabin. He never stayed to talk with Jane. He was too shy.

A month passed. One day Tarzan was alone at the cabin. Suddenly he heard Jane scream. Quickly he ran into the jungle.

The other men also heard the scream. They met Esmeralda coming from the jungle. "Mr. Porter! Mr. Porter!" she cried.

"Where is Jane? What happened?" asked Clayton.

"A great big ape took her away!" cried the maid.

The men ran into the jungle to search. They looked all day. They found nothing. When night came, they went back to the cabin. They knew they could find nothing in the dark.

The next day Clayton went outside. He could hardly believe his eyes. In the water was a ship. A small boat was heading for shore!

When it landed, some sailors came toward him. One of them spoke. "I am Captain d'Arnot. We are sailors in the French navy. We have come to take you home." Then d'Arnot told Clayton how he had captured their old ship. One of the sailors had told him about Professor Porter and the others. D'Arnot had looked for them for many days. Now he was ready to take them home.

Clayton should have been happy. But he was not.

"Miss Porter is missing," he said. "We can't leave without her. You must help us find her."

They all set off into the jungle.

But Jane had already been saved. Tarzan could follow the ape's tracks easily. All he had to do was look at the ground and at the trees. There was a bug, crushed by a heavy foot. A broken leaf and a bit of bark were other clues. Each clue was very tiny. However, Tarzan could follow them with great speed.

Soon he saw the ape. It was Terkoz, an ape from Tarzan's old tribe. He still held Jane in one hairy arm. Tarzan roared a challenge. Terkoz threw Jane aside. He turned to face Tarzan.

Tarzan and Terkoz came at each

other like charging bulls. They aimed
for each other's necks. Terkoz used
his teeth. Tarzan used his knife.
Before long Terkoz was dead.

Jane rushed to Tarzan. She threw her arms around him. Tarzan looked down at her. He kissed her.

Then Jane pushed him away. She could not understand her feelings. All she wanted was to stay in Tarzan's arms. She felt that she loved him more than anyone. However, Jane was a proper girl. Proper girls did not kiss strange men.

Tarzan was also confused. He loved Jane. He had loved her since the first day. He wanted to carry her away. That's what an ape would have done. But Tarzan was not an ape. He was a man. He knew he had to act differently.

So he cleared a place for Jane to sit. He gathered fruit and gave it to her. But he saw that she was still upset. Terkoz had scared her badly. Tarzan patted her hair. He quieted her as Kala had quieted him long ago. Then he took out his mother's locket. He kissed it and gave it to Jane.

Jane took the locket. She put it around her neck. Then Tarzan picked her up. She knew he was taking her back to the cabin. She did not really want to go! She felt so safe and happy in the jungle with Tarzan. But he was right. She had to go back.

For hours they swung through the trees. Tarzan traveled slowly. He wanted his time with Jane to last. Too soon the cabin was in front of them. Tarzan kissed Jane again. Then he heard something. Shots! He raced away to help.

It did not take Tarzan long to find the trouble. The sailors had run into some African warriors. The Africans thought the sailors were traders. Traders had attacked them in their old village. This time the Africans attacked first.

The fight was bloody. Many men were killed. The French picked up their wounded. They set off for the cabin. The Africans went back to their village. They had taken Captain d'Arnot prisoner. Tarzan headed for the village too. He knew that the prisoner would be in great danger.

When Tarzan got there, he saw d'Arnot. He was tied to a pole in the center of the village. He was badly hurt. Soon he would be dead. Tarzan

had to act fast! He threw his rope. It landed around a native's waist. He pulled hard. The native rose in the air. The night was very dark. The other natives could not see the rope. All they saw was a body flying in the air. The natives were scared. They ran to their huts. Now Tarzan had his chance. He jumped down. He untied d'Arnot and carried him away.

The Frenchman was too sick to travel. Tarzan had to stay with him in the jungle. Tarzan brought him food. He washed d'Arnot's wounds. Slowly d'Arnot got better.

When d'Arnot could sit up, Tarzan wrote a note. It said, "I am Tarzan of the Apes. Who are you? Can you read this?"

D'Arnot tried to answer out loud.

Tarzan shook his head. He gave d'Arnot the pencil. D'Arnot wrote, "I am Paul d'Arnot. I thank you for your help. You saved my life. Why can't you speak English? You write it so well."

Tarzan took the pencil and answered, "I speak as the apes do. I do not know how to speak to men. Will you teach me?"

So d'Arnot began lessons. He taught Tarzan French.

Tarzan learned very fast. By the time d'Arnot was able to travel, Tarzan could speak French well. Then the two men left for the cabin.

CHAPTER SIX

When d'Arnot and Tarzan got to the cabin, it was empty. Jane was gone. So were the French sailors. There was a note for Tarzan. With a sad heart, he read:

To Tarzan of the Apes:

Thank you for letting us use your cabin. I'm sorry I didn't meet you. There is another I would like to thank. I don't know his name. But I have his locket. If you know him, talk to him for me. Tell him I waited for him as long as I could. Until our boat had to sail. There was a terrible fight in the jungle. The captain, d'Arnot, died. His men came back with my father and Mr. Clayton. They wanted to leave. I had to go with them. Tell him I live in America. In Wisconsin. Tell him he may come if he wants. He will be welcome. Thank you again.

Jane Porter

Tarzan was very upset. He had come too late! He loved Jane. Now she was gone. D'Arnot was also sad. His men thought he was dead! His ship had sailed. He did not want to spend his life in the jungle.

Tarzan said, "How can we get to America?"

D'Arnot laughed. "It's too far. We would have to travel by ship."

"And where would we find a ship?" asked the ape man.

D'Arnot shook his head. "Far away. We would die crossing the jungle."

"I would rather die than stay here," said Tarzan. "Let us go."

"I will go with you," answered d'Arnot. "If we die, we die."

So Tarzan and d'Arnot began to walk. Their trip took months. On the way d'Arnot taught Tarzan many things. He showed Tarzan how to use a knife and fork. He explained how a gentleman acts. He taught Tarzan how to speak English.

Tarzan told d'Arnot about the chest Rat Face had buried. D'Arnot

knew it held a treasure. "If we live," said the Frenchman, "we will go back for the chest."

Tarzan also told d'Arnot about his childhood. He talked of his mother, Kala.

But d'Arnot broke in. "I don't believe Kala was your mother, Tarzan. You are not an ape."

"My father was a man," answered Tarzan. "But Kala was my mother."

"Perhaps your father was the man who lived in the cabin," said d'Arnot. "Wasn't there any clue there? Anything to tell you what had happened?"

"There is one special book," said Tarzan. "But I have never been able to read it."

Tarzan showed d'Arnot the diary. It was written in French. D'Arnot read it to Tarzan. When d'Arnot was done, he said, "That proves it. You are Lord Greystoke's son."

"No," said Tarzan. "The bones of a baby were in the cradle. That was his son."

But d'Arnot still believed that Tarzan was Greystoke's son. And he thought he could prove it. In the diary were some tiny fingerprints. Lord Greystoke's son had touched it with inky fingers. "If only I could have Tarzan's fingerprints studied," thought d'Arnot. "I'm sure they would be the same."

Soon d'Arnot and Tarzan came to a city. There they rented a boat. They sailed to the place where the treasure was. They dug up the chest of coins and sailed back to the city. Then they got on a big boat and headed for France.

In France, d'Arnot called a friend who was a policeman. "Take this man's fingerprints," he said. "Tell me if they are the same as the prints in this diary."

"I will let you know in a few

weeks," said the policeman.

But Tarzan did not want to wait. He wanted to see Jane! He left d'Arnot in France and sailed for America.

Jane had been home for months. She was very unhappy. She could not forget the handsome man of the jungle. But now she had to marry someone else. Robert Canler. She hated him. But her father owed him money. If Professor Porter did not pay it back, he would go to jail. By marrying Canler, Jane could save her father.

William Clayton stayed nearby. While he was in Africa, his father had died. He was now Lord Greystoke. And he was in love with Jane. He asked her to marry him. She had said no because of Canler. But Clayton would not give up hope.

The wedding day arrived. Jane went out for a walk in the woods. She wanted to be alone to think.

While she was out, a fire started in the forest near her house. Jane was so upset about Canler that she did not smell the smoke. Suddenly it was too late. The flames were all around her.

Just then a car pulled up to Jane's house. Tarzan got out. He was dressed in a dark suit. He looked like a perfect gentleman. Tarzan found William Clayton in Jane's house. Clayton had been sleeping. He did not know about the fire.

Clayton greeted Tarzan with the sad news. Jane would soon be married.

"Where is Jane?" asked Tarzan.

Clayton pointed outside. "She went for a walk."

Tarzan did not even answer. He saw the fire and ran toward the forest. The fire was spreading fast. No ordinary man could get through.

But Tarzan could. He swung through the tall trees. He cried,

"Jane Porter! Jane Porter!"

Jane heard him. "Here I am!" she screamed.

Tarzan dropped to the ground. Jane could hardly believe her eyes. The forest man, here in America! Come to save her again! Tarzan quickly carried Jane away from the fire. Then he set her down.

"Why didn't you come back to me?" said Jane. "I waited as long as I could."

"I was taking care of d'Arnot," answered Tarzan.

"I knew that was it . . . but . . . I do not even know your name. . . ."

"I was Tarzan of the Apes when we met. Now I am a gentleman." He turned away from her.

Then he said, "I heard you are to be married. To Robert Canler. Do you love him?"

"No!" said Jane in a loud voice. Then she explained about the money her father owed Canler.

"But I have brought your treasure. You are not poor anymore," said Tarzan.

Jane shook her head. "That is

wonderful news. But I have made a promise. I can ask Mr. Canler to go away. But if he says no, I must marry him anyway." She looked at Tarzan sadly. "If only we had had the money sooner . . . !"

Tarzan and Jane went back to the house. Everyone was surprised to see Tarzan.

Just then Canler arrived. "We can leave right now, Jane," he said. "Everything is ready for our wedding."

In a flash Tarzan's hand was on Canler's neck. It felt like a steel band. "You are trying to buy this woman," he said. "You know she does not want to marry you. I will give you your money. Take it—and your life—and go away."

There was fear in Canler's eyes. He hurried out of the room.

Jane was free. Now she could marry anyone she wanted. But whom did she want to marry? She had dreamed about Tarzan for many months. She thought she loved him. But she was not sure. He was a man of the jungle. He did not belong in a house or in a city. Could she be happy with him? Could she live in a jungle? She did not know.

Clayton wanted to marry her too. He was more like her. He had grown up in a city, like other men. She did not love him, but she did like him. Oh, what should she do?

All day Jane thought. In the evening Clayton came to see her. "Marry me, Jane," he said. "I can make you happy."

Jane looked at him for a long time. Then she said, "Yes. I know you can make me happy. I'll marry you."

Then she saw Tarzan. He was alone outside. She went to him.

Jane looked at Tarzan's face. It was a good, kind face. Suddenly she knew she was wrong. She *did* love him. She *could* be happy with Tarzan—anywhere. But again it was too late. Jane had given her word. She poured out her story to Tarzan. She told him everything—her thoughts, her fears, her love for him.

When she was done, Tarzan sighed. "I'll go away, Jane. I know your promise is important to you. I cannot ask you to break it."

Just then Clayton came in. He had a telegram. "This is for you, Tarzan," he said.

Tarzan read the telegram. It was from d'Arnot. It said, "Your fingerprints prove you are the son of Greystoke."

Tarzan looked at Clayton. This man was his cousin. All Clayton owned did not really belong to him. His lands, his title, and his money were really Tarzan's. Tarzan was the real Lord Greystoke! If Tarzan told him, Clayton would give up everything. He was a man of honor. But Jane was going to marry Clayton. She would also lose the land and the money. Tarzan did not want her to give up anything because of him.

Before Tarzan could say anything, Clayton spoke. "By the way, you never told us your story. How did you ever get into that jungle?"

"I was born there," Tarzan said. "My mother was an ape. She could not tell me much about it."

"And your father?" asked Clayton.

"I never knew who my father was," Tarzan said quietly. And just as quietly, he left them.

Edgar Rice Burroughs is one of the world's most popular authors. Between 1912 and 1950, he wrote 91 books as well as many short stories and articles. The best known of these are the 26 Tarzan novels, which have been translated into 32 languages.

Harold and **Geraldine Woods** are the authors of more than a dozen books, a dozen curriculum guides, and many magazine articles. Besides writing, they take turns teaching and staying home with their young son, Tommy. Tommy loves adventure stories and insisted on having the galleys of *Tarzan of the Apes* read to him three times. Harold and Geraldine Woods live in New York City.

Tim Gaydos has been an illustrator for the last 15 years, working primarily on book jackets. In his spare time he teaches at the Montclair Art Museum. *Tarzan of the Apes* is the first book he has illustrated for Random House. Mr. Gaydos lives in Montclair, New Jersey.